MISS BUTTERPAT
GOES WILD!

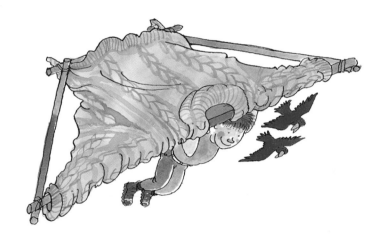

Malcolm Yorke

with illustrations by
Margaret Chamberlain

DORLING KINDERSLEY
LONDON • NEW YORK • STUTTGART

A DORLING KINDERSLEY BOOK

First published in Great Britain in 1994
by Dorling Kindersley Limited,
9 Henrietta Street, London WC2E 8PS

Reprinted 1994, 1996, 1997

A CIP catalogue record for this book is
available from the British Library

ISBN 0-7513-7014-2

Colour reproduction by DOT Gradations
Printed in Singapore

Miss Cushy Butterpat was a teacher. She sat in the school staffroom each lunchtime, sipping tea, nibbling coffee-creams, and knitting a large, blue sweater. All the staff and children thought she was a wonderful person, but perhaps a little bit dull.

It was the last day of the summer term and the long holidays were about to begin. Miss Butterpat said to her class:

"Now children, I hope you all have a lovely holiday and do lots of super things. When we meet again next term, I shall want to hear all about your adventures."

I'M GOING TO STAY ON MY UNCLE'S FARM.

WE'RE GOING TO FRANCE FOR OUR HOLIDAYS!

OUR COUSINS ARE COMING FROM CANADA.

AND MY AUNTIE'S COMING FROM TRINIDAD.

I'M GOING CAMPING IN SCOTLAND.

"Your plans sound wonderful," she said.

"What are you going to do, Miss?" asked Susan.

"Me? Oh well, I thought I might stow away on a ship to South America, explore the jungle, live with a tribe of Indians, canoe down the river – that sort of thing. …"

The class laughed and laughed.

"You do tell whoppers, Miss," said Leroy. And they all went off to their holidays, smiling at Miss Butterpat's little joke.

The next morning, Cushy Butterpat cut her hair very short and put on her jeans, some stout boots, and her big, blue sweater. She packed her rucksack and took the train to Liverpool.

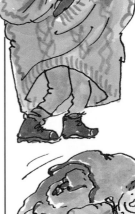

On the train, she went into the toilet. When she came out she was wearing a false beard and moustache.

She arrived in Liverpool where she met the captain of a cargo boat, the *Saucy Rachel*. She told the captain that her name was Charlie and that she would make a good deckhand on his voyage to South America.

"OK, join the crew," said the captain.

The other sailors thought Charlie was tough and hardworking. He could also play the tin whistle, drink rum, and play cards with the best of them.

The little cargo boat was tossed around by a wild typhoon, but at last it arrived safely in South America. Charlie helped to unload the cargo, said goodbye to the crew, and set off for the nearest town.

There was a carnival in town. Everybody was wearing fantastic costumes and parading through the streets. Cushy wanted to join in, so she threw away her beard and became Cushy Butterpat again.

She stretched her big, blue sweater and made herself look like a blue elephant by putting an arm down one sleeve for a trunk, and using the other for a tail.

"I know, I'll use some leaves for ears," thought Cushy. "And some rolled up paper for tusks."

She had a wonderful time in the parade and afterwards danced the rhumba, cha-cha-cha, and lambada until dawn.

The next day, Cushy caught a rusty
old steamboat up the local river.
As the boat went further and further
into the jungle, she could see the
monkeys and parrots in the trees
and hear the calls of the jaguars
and even the hiss of the snakes.

"This looks good," thought Cushy,
as she got off the boat. "I'm off to
explore the jungle."

OLD RUSTY

Cushy was feeling very hot in her big, blue sweater as she pushed her way through the leafy jungle. Suddenly, she was gripped by a huge boa constrictor. It began to coil round her, ready to squeeze her to death.

Fortunately, the blue sweater was so big and loose that Cushy was able to slip out of it before the squeeze got too tight. The puzzled snake found it had only an empty blue skin in its grip, so it slid off to find a less slippery victim.

Cushy Butterpat plodded on, nibbling berries and her supply of coffee-creams during the day, and camping out at night.

She came to another river. It was too wide and fast for her to swim across.

"How am I going to cross this?" Cushy wondered. "I know ..."

She took off her sweater and
pushed a branch through both arm
holes. She pushed other branches
across the sides and waist until it
looked like the sail of a hang-glider.
Then she jumped from a tree and ...
"Wheeeeee!"

She floated across the river perfectly,
but landed in a prickly bush on
the other side.

Cushy went on until she came to a village. The local Indians had never ever seen anyone like her before, but they were very friendly.

"You are a nice lady. You join our tribe?" they suggested.

"Thank you very much," said Cushy.

It was so hot in the village that Cushy didn't need her sweater any more. She unravelled part of it to make fishing lines. Another square of it was made into a butterfly net. Other bits went into necklaces or hair ribbons, and she taught the children how to play cat's cradle and fly a kite.

She joined her new friends when they fished and went hunting with spears and bows and arrows.

She helped to cook the food, amused the children, and was particularly good at playing the drums.

Eventually, Cushy remembered that she ought to be getting back home. The tribe was sad to see her go, but they gave her a canoe as a goodbye present.

"Bye bye, everyone," she called, and they cheered as she set off down the river.

For several days she paddled along the river. A crocodile fancied her for dinner. "Shoo," she said as she smacked it on the head with her paddle.

At the first big town, Cushy landed and sold her canoe. With the money she joined in a poker game. She played against a wicked bandit called Jake and managed to win his horse, saddle, a pistol, and a big bag of gold.

"I gonna getta you, lady," said the evil Jake, as he pointed his other pistol at her. But Cushy was quick. She shot a hole in his hat before he could even take aim.

Then she leaped on to the horse and galloped off out of town.

Eventually, Cushy reached the port again. She used her bag of gold to buy a first class ticket on an ocean liner bound for home.

What luxury! She sunbathed and swam in the pool, she ate delicious food, and every evening she danced!

"Marry me!" said all the men passengers who had fallen madly in love with her. They threatened to jump overboard if she did not dance with them. She told them all not to be so silly.

At last, Cushy reached Liverpool once again. She went to visit her granny and spent the last few days of her holiday mowing her granny's lawn and weeding her garden.

Every afternoon they had tea and coffee creams whilst Granny told Cushy all the local gossip. Her old gran did not once ask Cushy how she had spent the rest of her holiday.

When Cushy Butterpat went back to school the other teachers were very chatty.

MY, YOU LOOK BROWN, CUSHY!

I'M NOT SURE THAT NEW HAIRSTYLE SUITS YOU.

YOU'VE LOST A BIT OF WEIGHT.

Then they all told her about their holidays in Bognor Regis, Spain, and Scarborough. Nobody bothered to ask Miss Butterpat what **she'd** been doing all summer.

Cushy's class told her all about **their** holidays.

I SAW COWS BEING MILKED.

I LEARNED HOW TO COUNT TO TEN IN FRENCH.

OUR COUSINS HAVE GOT FUNNY CANADIAN ACCENTS.

MY AUNTIE COOKED US REAL WEST INDIAN FOOD!

Miss Butterpat listened to them all with great interest. Then Susan said, "And what did **you** do, Miss?"

"Me? Oh well, I wore a beard and pretended to be a sailor, took part in a carnival as a blue elephant, escaped from a boa constrictor, made a hang-glider, and …"

They all laughed and laughed.

YOU'RE HAVING US ON AGAIN!

IT'S NOT STORYTIME YET, MISS!

GO ON, MISS, NOW TELL US WHAT YOU REALLY DID.

"Well, I stayed with my granny and mowed her lawn and weeded her garden," said Miss Cushy Butterpat with a sigh.

"That's more like it," the children said. This time they believed her.

That same lunchtime Miss Butterpat
sat in the staffroom, sipping her tea
and nibbling her coffee-creams again.
She also began to knit another huge
sweater. This time a red one.

It would keep her warm next
year when she climbed Everest.